W9-ACP-534

Text copyright © 2012
by Harriet Ziefert
Illustrations copyright © 2012
by Travis Foster
All rights reserved /
CIP Data is available.
Published in the United States
2012 by
🍎Blue Apple Books,
515 Valley Street
Maplewood, NJ 07040
www.blueapplebooks.com
First Edition 10/12
Printed in Shenzhen, China
ISBN: 978-1-60905-250-8

2 4 6 8 10 9 7 5 3 1

The Princess and...

THE Peas AND Carrots

BY Harriet Ziefert

ILLUSTRATIONS BY Travis Foster

BLUE APPLE

for Sylvie Ann Ziefert
—HZ

Once upon a time, there was a little girl
who liked everything just so.
Her name was Rosebud.

In the morning, Rosebud made her bed, then arranged
her stuffed animals on the pillows.

She chose her own outfits and was quite particular about what she wore.
Nothing itchy. Nothing woolly. Everything soft . . .
and preferably in pink or purple.

When Rosebud went to her art table,
first she lined up her crayons. Then she began to draw.

If she made a mistake,
Rosebud crumpled her paper and
started over on a clean sheet.

Rosebud loved to play dress-up.
Her favorite costume was a pink satin gown.
She wore it with purple plastic slippers,
gold bangle bracelets, and a silver crown.

When she paraded in front of her father, he announced,

"Here comes the Good Princess Rosebud!"

But Good Princess Rosebud wasn't always good.

If sand got inside her bathing suit,
she insisted on a change of clothes.

If snow drifted into her boots, she complained.

If there was a little hole in her tights . . .

a little wrinkle in her sock . . .

a little pebble in her sneakers . . .

a little label in the collar of her shirt . . .

she fussed.

Her mother said,
"From now on, I'm calling you
PRINCESS FUSSY!"

Mealtime could be difficult.
If there were lumps in her oatmeal,
Rosebud yelled.

If there were seeds in the grapes,
or pits in the watermelon,
she pushed her plate away.

If there were greens in the noodle soup,
Rosebud insisted they be removed.

Her big brother yelled,
"Stop fussing
and EAT!"

At one family dinner, Rosebud's mother served roast chicken,
mashed potatoes with gravy, and peas and carrots.

Rosebud glared at her plate.
The peas were touching the carrots,
the chicken was on top
of the mashed potatoes,
and the gravy
was touching everything!

Rosebud shoved her plate away with both hands.
She was as surprised as everyone
when her entire meal landed on the floor.
What a mess!

Her mother said,
"I've had enough, Miss Fussy!
Leave this table and go right to your room!"

Rosebud threw her stuffed animals onto the floor.

Then she tossed the pillows . . . the quilt . . . and the blanket.

Rosebud **kicked,** and
Rosebud **screamed**.

Rosebud's mommy and daddy heard her cries.
"If—and only if—you stop screaming, we will help you."

Rosebud calmed down.
She said she was sorry for making a mess—
in the kitchen and in her room.

Rosebud wanted food.
And a nice, neat bed
to sleep in.

Rosebud's mommy straightened the sheet,
fluffed the pillow, and remade the bed.
She checked under the mattress
and found a tennis ball and a pink sock.

Rosebud arranged her animals
just the way she liked them.
She ate peas and carrots. And chicken, too.

Then Daddy said, "I'll tell you the story of a princess and a pea."

Daddy began.

Once upon a time there was a prince
who wanted to marry a real princess. He met many princesses,
but it was hard to tell which one was real.

There was something about each princess that did not seem right.
Though they said they were princesses, the prince did not believe them.

The king and queen arranged for a secret test.
They asked their servants to hide a pea underneath 20 mattresses.
In order to make the test even harder,
20 feather beds were added atop the mattresses.

One day a wet and soggy princess came to the palace.
She said she was the real deal and asked to spend the night.

By the middle of the story, Rosebud's eyes began
to close. She was sleepy. So was her daddy!

"Please finish the story, Daddy," mumbled Rosebud.
"Don't go to sleep yet."

The Queen thought, *Who else but a real princess could detect a tiny pea under 40 layers?*

So the next night, the queen ordered her servants to give the soggy princess
the most comfortable bed in the palace and
she finally got a good night's sleep.

Rosebud tried to go to sleep, too.

But she **tossed** . . .

and **turned**.

So she got out of bed . . .

and whispered, "Daddy, I can't sleep.
There's a lump in my bed."

Rosebud's sleepy daddy got up from his chair. He checked her bed.
And what do you think he found? A marble!

Who else but a real princess could detect a tiny marble
under all those sheets and blankets?

Nobody but our Rosebud,
a real princess, too!

2 1982 02804 1261